An Alligator Ate My Brother

by **Mary Olson**

Illustrated by **Tammie Lyon**

Text copyright © 2000 by Mary Olson
Illustrations copyright © 2000 by Tammie Lyon
All rights reserved

Published by Caroline House
Boyds Mills Press, Inc.
A Highlights Company
815 Church Street
Honesdale, Pennsylvania 18431
Printed in China

Publisher Cataloging-in-Publication Data

Olson, Mary.
    An alligator ate my brother / by Mary Olson ; illustrated by
Tammie Lyon.—1st ed.
[32]p. : col. ill. ;   cm.
Summary: No one believes a young boy when he says an alligator is in the house.
ISBN 1-56397-803-2
1. Alligators—Fiction—Juvenile literature. 2. Brothers—Fiction—Juvenile literatur
[1. Alligators—Fiction.   2. Brothers—Fiction.]
I. Lyon, Tammie, ill. II. Title.
    [E] — dc21   2000   AC   CIP
98-89692

First edition, 2000
The text of this book is set in 16-point Berkeley.
The illustrations are done in watercolor.
Visit us on the World Wide Web: www.boydsmillspress.com

10 9 8 7 6 5 4 3 2 1

To my husband and sons with love.

—M. W. O.

For Lee, who is always supportive;
for Jake, who warns me of deliveries;
and for Moe, who faithfully sleeps in front of my desk every day.
I love you guys.

—T. L.

It was almost time for dinner. My mother was mashing potatoes. My father was flipping hamburgers. My sister, Lydia, was writing a book report. I was fixing my fire engine. Suddenly, we heard a loud thump from the end of the hall.

"Paul, see if Jimmy's okay," said my mother. My brother, Jimmy, is always getting into trouble. I ran to the playroom.

"Jimmy's fine," I shouted. "But an alligator just climbed through the playroom window!"

My mother said, "Uh-huh," and kept right on mashing potatoes.

Scuffle, scuffle, scuffle, boom!

My father looked up. "Paul, see if Jimmy's still in one piece," he said.

I galloped back to the kitchen. "He's still in one piece," I panted. "But that alligator is chasing him all over the house!"

My father shook his head and flipped another hamburger.
Slither, rattle, rattle, bang!

Lydia said, "Paul, see if Jimmy needs help putting away his blocks." She's so bossy.

I raced to the bedroom and found Jimmy running as fast as he could, one step ahead of the alligator. "*Slurp!*" The alligator swallowed Jimmy's blocks. "*Slurp!*" The alligator ate Jimmy's bear. I tore back to the kitchen.

"Jimmy doesn't need help with his blocks!" I exclaimed. "He needs help fighting off that alligator!"

My mother smiled. My father winked. Lydia crossed her eyes.

"Slurp, slurp, slurrppp!"

Everyone looked up. "Paul, see what Jimmy has gotten into now!"

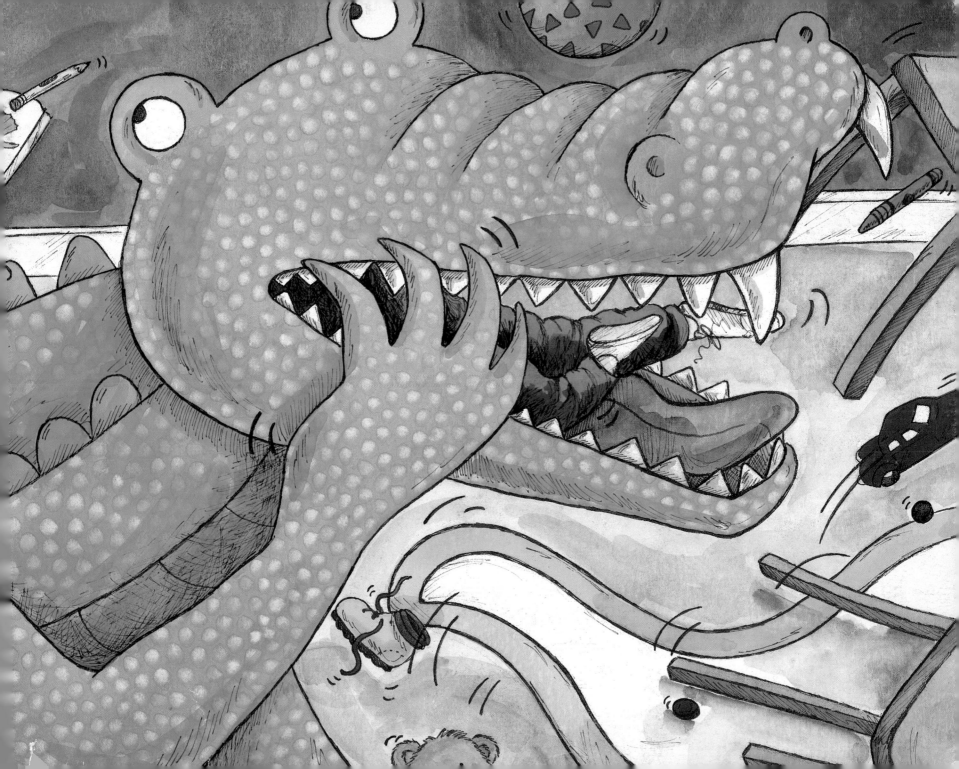

"He's gone," I said. "He must be in the alligator's stomach!" No one moved. "An alligator ate my brother! Don't you care?"

"Of course we do," said my mother. "Now bring Jimmy in for dinner."

I ran back to Jimmy's bedroom. There was no sign of him—just a big, fat, happy alligator snoring in the corner.

"I'll save you, Jimmy!" I yelled.

I leaped onto my brother's bed. "Yee-haa!" I cried and jumped on the alligator's stomach.

"*Umpppph!*" burped the alligator. Out came the blocks.
Out came the teddy bear. And out came Jimmy.
I grabbed my brother's hand and ran.

"Help, help, help!" shouted Jimmy.
"Get help," I cried, "before that alligator eats all of us!"
Everyone smiled.
Boom!
A sudden crash shook the house. My mother put down her
fork. My father put down his spatula. Lydia forgot all about her
book report.

They ran down the hall searching every room.
The alligator was nowhere in sight.

"See," said Lydia, sticking out her tongue, "there
is no alligator." She marched to the kitchen.

"You've got to stop making up stories like this,"
said my father.

"Especially about alligators," my mother added.

"Slurp, slurp, slurp!"

"What was that?" asked my parents.

"Oh, no," I said. "I think an alligator ate my sister!"
I ran to the kitchen.

Disappearing out the kitchen door was a long green tail.

"Don't worry, Lydia, I'll save you! Yee-haa!"

Peach
Girl

· Story by Raymond Nakamura ·

· Illustrations by Rebecca Bender ·

pajama press

First published in the United States in 2014
Text copyright © Raymond Nakamura
Illustration copyright © Rebecca Bender
This edition copyright © 2014 Pajama Press Inc.

This is a first edition.

10 9 8 7 6 5 4 3 2 1

www.pajamapress.ca   info@pajamapress.ca

Canada Council   Conseil des arts
for the Arts   du Canada

ONTARIO ARTS COUNCIL
CONSEIL DES ARTS DE L'ONTARIO

The publisher gratefully acknowledges the support of the Canada Council for the Arts and the Ontario Arts Council for its publishing program. We acknowledge the financial support of the Government of Canada through the Canada Book Fund for our publishing activities.

Library and Archives Canada Cataloguing in Publication

Nakamura, Raymond, 1962-, author   Peach girl / story by Raymond Nakamura ; art by Rebecca Bender.

ISBN 978-1-927485-58-3 (bound)

    I. Bender, Rebecca, illustrator II. Title.

PS8627.A534P42 2014   jC813'.6   C2013-907852-5

Publisher Cataloging-in-Publication Data (U.S.)

Nakamura, Raymond, 1962-

    Peach girl / story by Raymond Nakamura ; art by Rebecca Bender.

[32] pages : col. ill. ; cm.

Summary: In this reimagining of a Japanese folk tale, Momoko is born from a peach to make the world a better place. Despite rumors of a terrible ogre that lives nearby and eats children, Momoko bravely sets out with a pocketful of dumplings and the timid Monkey, Dog, and Pheasant to find out the truth for herself.

ISBN-13: 978-1-927485-58-3

1. Folklore – Japan. I. Bender, Rebecca, 1980-, illustrator. II. Momotaro. III. Title. 398.22 dc23
PZ8.1.N343Pe   2014

The original art is painted in acrylics on illustration board, prepared with a textured surface.
The text is set in Myster Text and Myster Bold.
Edited by Ann Featherstone
Designed by Rebecca Bender

Manufactured by Friesens. Printed in Canada.

Pajama Press Inc.
112 Berkeley St., Toronto, Ontario, Canada, M5A 2W7
www.pajamapress.ca

Distributed in the U.S. by Orca Book Publishers
PO Box 468, Custer, WA, 98240-0468, USA

For Risa, of course
    ~R.N.

For my parents, who are as
peachy as they come
    ~R.B.

One morning in old Japan, a farmer and her husband found a great big peach at their door.

"Well I never...," said the farmer. "We only grow radishes."

"I'm hungry," said the husband.

"Then let's cut it open," said the farmer.

But before the farmer could fetch a knife, the peach split apart and a girl hopped out.

"Hello," she said. "My name is Momoko. I'm here to make the world a better place."

"Well, I never...," said the farmer. "But it's cold out there. You need some clothes."

The farmer and her husband brought the girl and the peach inside. The farmer peeled the skin off the peach to make clothes for the girl.

"Peachy," said Momoko. "Now I'm ready to go."

"But I've heard there's an ogre out there who eats small children," said the husband. "You need some protection."

The husband turned the halves of the peach pit into a helmet and shield.

"Peachy," said Momoko. "Now I'm ready to go."

"But you might get hungry out there," said the farmer. "You need some food."

So the farmer cut up the peach to make dumplings.

"Peachy," said Momoko. "Now I'm ready to go."

"But—," the husband started to say.

Momoko hugged the couple and said, "Thanks for all your help, Mom and Dad. Now I'm off to find the ogre and make the world a better place."

The husband waved goodbye with a tear in his eye.

"They grow up so quickly," said the farmer.

Soon Momoko came to a forest, where she met a monkey.

"Honorable Monkey, have you seen an ogre around here?"

"I've heard he lives in the village," said the monkey.

"If you help me find him, I'll share my dumplings with you."

"But he's bigger than a tree and he eats small children."

"Well, if you are afraid, I can find him myself."

"No, no," said the monkey. "I will help you. Those dumplings sure sound good."

"Peachy," said Momoko.

Soon they came to the village, where they met a dog.

"Honorable Dog, have you seen an ogre around here?" asked Momoko.

"I've heard he lives by the lake," said the dog.

"If you help us find him, we will share our dumplings with you."

"But he has teeth like knives and he eats small children."

"Well, if you are a scaredy-cat," said the monkey, "all the more dumplings for us."

"I am no cat," said the dog. "I will help you. Those dumplings sure smell good."

"Peachy," said Momoko.

Soon they came to the lake, where they met a pheasant.

"Honorable Pheasant, have you seen an ogre around here?" asked Momoko.

"I've heard he lives in the castle on that island," said the pheasant.

"If you help us get there, we will share our dumplings with you."

"But he has eyes that shoot flames and he eats small children."

"Well, if you are chicken," said the dog, "all the more dumplings for us."

"I am no chicken," said the pheasant. "I will help you. Those dumplings sure look good."

"Peachy," said Momoko. "Now we need a boat."

Momoko took off her peach pits to use as floats. The monkey gathered reeds. The dog fetched some sticks. The pheasant picked up old feathers. And together they built a boat strong enough to carry them all.

Filled with courage, they set off for the island.

The monkey said, "I could unlock the gate."

The dog said, "Or I could dig under it."

And the pheasant said, "Or I could fly over it."

"Peachy," said Momoko. "Thank you all *for* helping me look *for* the ogre—even though he might be bigger than a tree, have teeth like knives, have eyes that shoot *flames*, and eat small children."

The animals became quiet.

When they landed, the monkey shook too much
to pick the lock.

The dog shivered too much to dig under the gate.

And the pheasant quaked too much to *fly* over it.

So Momoko clanked the metal door knocker.

Clank, clank, clank.

After some time, a grumbly voice said, "Who is it?"

"This is Momoko and I am here with my friends—Monkey, Dog, and Pheasant."

"Well, I never...," the voice said. "Are you, by any chance, bigger than a tree?"

"No," said the monkey.

"Do you have teeth like knives?"

"No," said the dog.

"What about eyes that shoot flames?"

"No," said the pheasant.

"What about you?" asked Momoko.

"Certainly not," said the voice.

"We have peach dumplings," said Momoko.

"Peach dumplings!"

The gate swung open and out stepped an ogre who was bigger than a bush, with teeth like chopsticks and eyes that glowed with warmth.

He said with a big smile, "Come in, come in! You're just in time for tea."

"You don't eat small children, do you?" Momoko asked.

"Certainly not," said the ogre.

"Peachy," said Momoko.

"These dumplings are yummy," said the ogre, and everyone agreed. "You must come again. I do get lonely here all by myself."

Momoko smiled. "Next time, I'll bring my folks too."

"Peachy," said the ogre.